About the Book

Baseball is the No. 1 game in America. The tens of millions who watch or play the game take it very seriously.

Here is a book that will help young readers understand baseball better. It explains the basic rules, equipment, game strategy, and how major, minor, and amateur leagues are structured. There are tips on how to hit and how to pitch. A section explains how to figure batting, fielding, and pitching averages. Another defines baseball's words and terms.

A bit of history is included, plus a rundown of the major awards to players today. Statistical charts give American League and National League divisions, team moves in recent years, major league stadiums, and records for major league leaders in ten different categories.

A companion book to *All About Football*.

ALL ABOUT
BASEBALL

George Sullivan

Illustrated with photographs and diagrams

G. P. Putnam's Sons   New York

Copyright © 1989 by George Sullivan.
All rights reserved.
Published simultaneously in Canada.
Printed in the United States of America.

Library of Congress Cataloging-in-Publication Data
Sullivan, George, 1928– All about baseball.
Includes index. 1. Baseball—United States. I. Title.
GV863.A1S89 1989 796.357'0973 88-29716
ISBN 0-399-61226-2 (HC)
1 3 5 7 9 10 8 6 4 2

ISBN 0-399-21734-7 (PBK)
15 17 19 20 18 16 14

Frontispiece: Joe DiMaggio, the Yankee Clipper, won two American League batting championships and two MVP titles. He retired after the 1951 season with a career batting average of .325.

The author is grateful to the many people who contributed information and photographs for use in this book. Special thanks are due: Larry Shenk, Philadelphia Phillies; Dan Ewald, Detroit Tigers; Howard Starkman, Toronto Blue Jays; Harvey Greene and Lou D'Ermilio, New York Yankees; Dick Bresciani, Boston Red Sox; M. Scott Smith, Rawlings; Francesca Kurti, TLC Custom Labs; Carole and Jack Moran, and Brendan McGowan.

Contents

Introduction

In mid-February, when the excitement of the Super Bowl has faded, baseball's spring training begins. From that time until the World Series is decided late in October, baseball is king. Of course, there's also pro basketball and pro hockey during this time. But neither compares with baseball.

Baseball is special. The tens of millions of people who watch the game or play it take baseball very seriously.

Early in April, once the major league season starts, baseball never goes away. Fans have only a few hours to discuss one game before another is underway.

Baseball may be the No. 1 game in America because it is so easy to appreciate. Everything is spread out over a couple of acres. You can follow the ball everywhere and see big plays developing—a pinch-hitter swinging a couple of bats in the on-deck circle, a runner taking a long lead off second base.

You can follow baseball on television. You can also follow

it on radio, where a skilled announcer can help you create the game in your head.

Of course, there are millions who, besides being fans, also play the game. There are teams and leagues for players of every age.

The term "players" used to refer only to boys and men. But during the 1970s, girls and women began to play the game. They now participate on school and Little League teams.

Baseball has spread far beyond America's borders. The game is now played in Canada, Italy, Japan, Korea, Taiwan, the Philippines, the Netherlands, South Africa, and most Latin American nations. In 1987, the Russians gave it a try.

This book will help you to understand baseball better. It explains the basic rules and game strategy. It tells you how baseball is organized and how to figure a batting average (your own or your favorite player's). There are some playing tips for pitchers and hitters. You'll find that the more you know about the game, the more fun you'll get from it. So read and enjoy.

1

Some Basics

In trying to understand the game of football, the first step is to try to learn the many confusing terms that players, coaches, and broadcasters use. There is the "flex" defense, the double-double, and the 4-3 and 3-4, plus scores of other and similar terms for formations and plays.

In baseball, it's different. There's no mumbo jumbo. When the first baseman moves up, closer to home plate, because he thinks the batter may be going to bunt, the move isn't given any fancy name. The first baseman is said to be "playing in." Most other baseball terms are just as easy to understand.

Let's begin with the basics. Baseball is a game played with a bat and ball by opposing teams of nine players each. The teams take turns batting and playing in the field. The players at bat have to run a route of four bases that are laid out in a square in order to score a run.

The field is divided into three sections: the infield, the outfield, and foul territory. The infield is covered with dirt;

the outfield is grass. Some parks with artificial turf in both the infield and outfield have a painted white line that divides the two.

The team on defense has four players stationed around the infield. They are: a first baseman near first base, a second baseman between first and second base, a third baseman near third base, and a shortstop between third base and second base.

There are three players stationed in the outfield: a left fielder, center fielder, and right fielder.

A pitcher in approximately the middle of the infield pitches to a catcher who is behind home plate.

The batter represents the opposing team. He stands to the left or right of home plate, tries to hit the ball as hard and as far as possible without being put out.

Two foul lines divide fair territory from foul territory. The foul lines meet at home plate where they form a right angle. They extend from the plate into the outfield all the way to the fence.

At the fence, each foul line extends straight up a towering foul pole. The foul pole helps to determine whether a ball blasted out of the field of play is a home run or merely a foul ball.

The foul lines and the foul poles are in fair territory. This means that any ball that touches a foul line is a fair ball. Any ball that caroms off a foul pole is a home run.

Foul-line pole and screen attached to it are in fair territory.

The Infield

The infield is a square area with a base at each corner. Each base is 90 feet from the next one (60 feet in Little League play).

Each is 15 inches square. Bases are held in place by one of two methods: by a flat-sided post attached to the under-

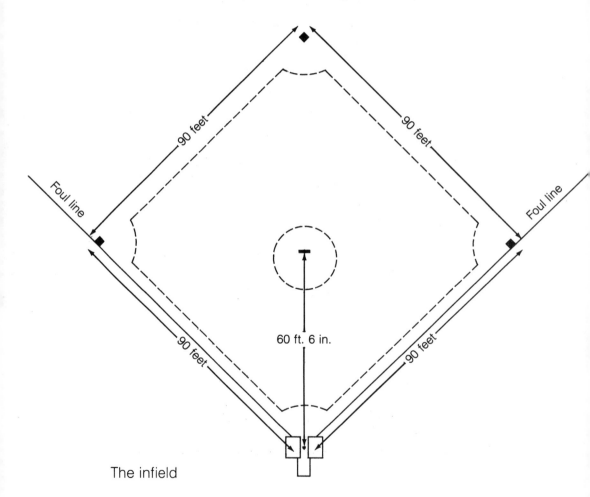

The infield

side of the base frame that fits into a short pipe sunk in the ground, or by wide straps that fasten to brackets anchored in the ground.

In the case of first and third bases, the outer edges of each meet the foul line. Thus, the entire base is in fair territory, and any ball that hits a base is fair. Of course, second base is in fair territory too.

Home plate is a five-sided slab of rubbery material that is anchored in the ground by long spikes. The plate's top surface is level with the ground.

On either side of the plate, chalk lines mark the boundaries of a rectangular-shaped batter's box. One is for right-handed batters, the other for left-handers.

The batter is supposed to stand inside the box. But many batters like to stand very deep in the box, so they have more time to eye the pitch. As a result, the back line of the box gets rubbed out. When this happens, a batter's rear foot may go beyond the line.

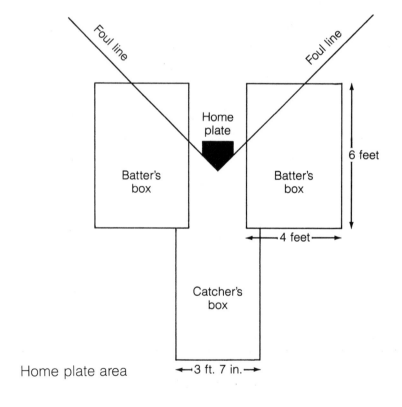

Home plate area

Groundskeeper puts down the circular white line that encloses home plate and batters' boxes. Scene is Yankee training camp in Fort Lauderdale, Florida.

A third rectangle, the catcher's box, is marked off directly behind home plate. The catcher must stay within this box while awaiting the pitch.

Other white lines outline the two rectangular coach's boxes, one near first base, the other near third base. The coaches who occupy these boxes help direct strategy on the base paths.

Of the two, the third base coach is the more important. It is the third base coach who usually receives hand signals from the manager during the game, and relays them to the batters and base runners.

The on-deck circles are also marked off in white chalk. There are two of them, each 5 feet in diameter. Each is located between a dugout and home plate. The batter due to bat next waits in the on-deck circle.

The field also includes two bullpens, one for each team. Often located in a fenced-in area beyond the outfield, the bullpens are occupied by the relief pitchers and their catcher. It's where the relievers warm up.

Where did the term "bullpen" originate? According to one theory, the outfield fences in baseball parks were often used to advertise Bull Durham chewing tobacco. A connection developed between the signs and the pitchers who were warming up near the outfield boundaries.

The players' benches are enclosed in dugouts located in foul territory on each side of the infield. The dugout floor is usually several feet lower than ground level, so the dugout itself will not block the view of the spectators. Each dugout is usually linked by a tunnel or corridor to the dressing room.

The Outfield

Football is always played on a field of standard size. One tennis court is exactly the same as any other. But in baseball the size and shape of the outfield varies from ballpark to ballpark.

One rule concerning ballpark size says that in the case of parks opened before June 1, 1958, the fences at the foul lines must be at least 250 feet from home plate. For ball parks opened after that date, the distance must be at least 325 feet down each foul line and at least 400 feet in center field.

Fenway Park, home grounds for the Boston Red Sox, is well known for its short fences. In left field, it's only 315 feet to the wall, to the "Green Monster," as it is called. In right field, the distance is even less, 302 feet. It's no wonder that the Red Sox usually lead the American League in home-park homers and runs scored.

The outcome of games at Boston's Fenway Park is often influenced by towering left-field wall, the "Green Monster."

Chicago's Comiskey Park has the longest lines in the American League—347 feet down both the right- and left-field lines. Through the years, home runs have been relatively rare in Comiskey Park. The Astrodome in Houston and Royals Stadium in Kansas City are other stadiums with what players call "downtown fences."

Playing Surfaces

It's not only the size of the park that's important. Also critical is what the surface is made of—real grass or the artificial kind. As of 1988, four of the fourteen teams in the American League played on artificial turf, also known as AstroTurf, its trade name. Six of the twelve teams in the National League played on the synthetic stuff. (See chart, page 80.)

Most players don't like artificial turf. Batted balls shoot through the infield in the blink of an eye. Infielders complain that being a skilled gloveman isn't really necessary on fake grass. What is important is being positioned properly before the pitch, because there's little time to react.

Outfield play is different, too. A sharply hit ball can easily scoot past the outfielders and go all the way to the wall. An inside-the-park home run can be the result. Outfielders have to play very deep, keeping as much of the field visible as possible. And they have to be certain to back up one another.

Players can run faster on the "carpeted" fields but bunt-

Houston's Astrodome, first park to use artificial turf.

ing is a problem. The fast-rolling ball always seems to go right to an infielder.

Artificial turf has been used in the major leagues since 1966, the year it was installed in the Houston Astrodome, a covered stadium that opened in 1965. During its first year of operation, the Astrodome faced a serious problem. The infield and outfield grass turned yellow and died. Spraying the grass with green paint didn't help matters. The paint got on the baseball and players' uniforms. When the season was over, Houston officials started looking for a grass substitute. That's when they discovered the synthetic grass they came to call AstroTurf.

After a downpour, artificial turf can be vacuumed dry with a Zamboni water removal machine.

2

Ball, Bat, and Glove

In baseball's earliest days, players played bare-handed. The first gloves didn't make their appearance until 1875, more than twenty-five years after baseball was invented.

The first bats were borrowed from cricket, also a ball and bat game. But in cricket the bat is flat-sided. Round bats were introduced to baseball in 1862.

Bases used to be four-feet-high stakes. But since players were often injured running into the stakes, they were replaced by flat rocks. The rocks caused injuries, too. They were discarded in favor of cloth bags filled with sand, which led to the bases of the present day.

The Baseball

The baseball is 9 to 9¼ inches in circumference and weighs between 5 and 5¼ ounces. Its cork-ball center is enclosed in rubber and tightly wound with layers of cotton and wool yarn. There are 150 yards of cotton yarn, and 219 yards of wool yarn.

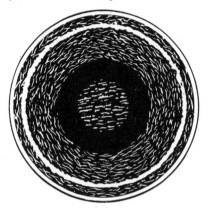

Major league baseballs have a cushioned cork center surrounded by layers of wool and cotton yarn.

The ball has a hide cover. It used to be horsehide. But since 1974, the cover has been cowhide. Also in 1974, the Rawlings Company took over from Spalding as the baseball manufacturer for the major leagues.

Cowhide baseball covers are produced for Rawlings by the Tennessee Tanning Company in Tullahoma, Tennessee. The two cover pieces, each shaped like the figure 8, are sewn together by hand with exactly 108 stitches.

The Bat

The rules for major league baseball say that the bat can be no more than 42 inches long and 2¾ inches in diameter at its thickest point. It must be made of wood.

The best bat wood is white ash, found in the forests of Pennsylvania and northern New York. White ash is strong

Bat "billets" await weighing and grading before being transformed into weapons for major league sluggers.

and hard, yet it has some "give" to it. This enables an ash bat to absorb the shock of smacking a baseball traveling at 90 or so miles an hour.

The rules concerning bats overlook one of the most important developments in the past twenty-years—the aluminum bat. How widespread is the use of aluminum bats? Well, at one time, Hillerich & Bradsby of Lousiville, Ken-

Billets are cut and shaped to hitter's specifications.

tucky, the leading manufacturer, was making six million wooden bats a year. Because aluminum bats have become so popular, the company now turns out only a million or so wooden bats a year.

While aluminum bats cost more than wood, they almost never break. They're used at every level of the game—except the major leagues.

Baseball officials fear that the use of aluminum bats by major leaguers would trigger big changes in the game. They might help to produce many more hits and an outpouring of 500-foot home runs. Aluminum bats could aid in wiping out the game's hitting records. So don't look for your favorite major league slugger to be swinging an aluminum bat anytime in the near future.

A major league player may use as many as sixty or seventy bats in a season. Teams must pay for their bats. They cost about $10 apiece.

Many major league players prefer using a cup-ended bat. These "hollowed-out" bats were first used in Japan. They became popular in the major leagues during the late 1970s. The idea is that you swing faster when using a bat with a top that has been hollowed out.

Other recent trends have been the use of pine tar on the bat handle and the wearing of batting gloves to improve the grip.

One other hitting aid must be mentioned, and that's corking, which is illegal. Corking is to hitting what scuffing the ball or applying spit is to pitching.

In corking a bat, the top is drilled out for a distance of from 6 to 8 inches. Another and lighter material—usually cork—is then substituted in place of the wood. Corking, like using a cup-ended bat, is said to give a faster swing.

When Craig Nettles played for the New York Yankees, he was caught with a corked bat. It happened during the season of 1974. After Nettles swung and hit the ball, the top flew off to reveal the cork-filled barrel. The only penalty for using an illegal bat is that the player is called out—which is what happened to Nettles.

Gloves

Besides a bat and ball, you need a glove to play the game. There are three kinds—the catcher's mitt, the first baseman's mitt, and the fielder's glove worn by outfielders and the other infielders.

Catchers use a fourth type of mitt. It's the oversize mitt that they get out whenever a knuckle-ball pitcher takes the mound. When trying to glove the tricky knuckler, the big mitt helps.

Most major league players have several gloves. One is for everyday use. Another is brand-new, waiting to be used. A third is being broken in, that is, being made ready for daily use.

When breaking in a glove, a player will take a little bit of hot water and rub it into the glove's pocket, then have a teammate throw hard to him until the pocket deepens and becomes set. Or the player will put a baseball in the wet pocket, wrap the glove tightly and let it dry slowly.

Once the pocket is set, a couple of drops of castor oil are rubbed over the leather. A liquid preparation called Lexol is often used inside the glove to keep the leather soft and flexible.

Uniforms

The New York Knickerbockers, a team that played as early as 1845, are believed to be the first team to wear

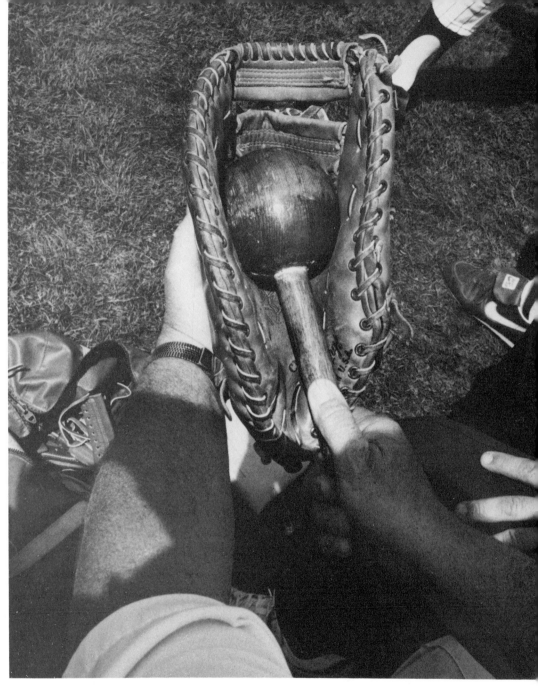

Major leaguers sometimes use a glove pounder to help form a pocket in a new glove.

baseball uniforms. In 1851, the Knickerbockers appeared for a game outfitted in long dark-blue trousers, webbed belts, white shirts, and straw hats.

In 1868, the Cincinnati Red Stockings introduced pants that were gathered and banded just below the knee, called knickerbockers, or knickers, for short. Opposing players laughed and jeered at the Red Stockings. But in a short time knee-length pants became standard for all teams.

If you've seen photographs of baseball players from the 1940s or 1950s or earlier, you can tell at a glance that uniforms were quite different then. Baggy uniforms were in style. Now, of course, they're tight fitting, a style that was pioneered by Willie Mays when he played for the San Francisco Giants during the 1960s.

Besides being loose fitting, uniforms of the recent past had no bright colors; they were either white or gray. In 1962, the Kansas City Athletics introduced green and gold uniforms. Other players hooted at the A's. But by the 1970s, most other teams were wearing bright colors, too.

Other Equipment

Batting helmets are as much a part of the game today as scoreboard videos and pine-tar rags. But baseball was played for about a century before players made any attempt to protect their heads from pitched balls.

On September 15, 1952, the Pittsburgh Pirates introduced helmets. The players were made to wear them all

These helmets and
bats belong to the
Toronto Blue Jays.

the time, not just when at bat. After a few years, the Pirates decided their players didn't have to wear their helmets in the field, only on trips to the plate.

The early helmet had no earflap. The earflap was developed in Little League play and copied by the major leagues.

Catchers need special equipment. This includes a heavy

John Russell, a catcher for the Phillies, snaps on his leg protection.

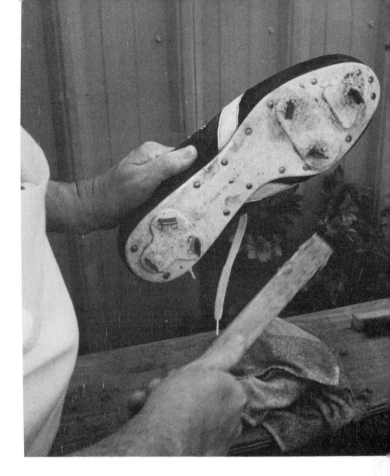

For games on natural grass, players wear cleats like these.

metal mask, a chest protector that covers the chest and belly, and hard-plastic shin guards to protect the legs. The catcher also wears a helmet. It's similar to the batting helmet except that it has no peak.

The catcher's mask has a flap hanging from it to protect the throat. The flap was first used by Steve Yeagher in 1977 after he got hit in the throat that year by a flying bat.

The shoes worn by players have spikes in the soles. Those who play on real grass and dirt wear shoes with metal spikes. Players who perform on artificial turf wear shoes fitted with hard-plastic spikes.

3

About Pitching

When a game begins, a player from the visiting team takes his position in the batter's box. The pitcher goes into his windup and delivers the ball. The batter tries to hit it with his bat. The game of baseball is based upon this matchup.

Of the two opponents, it's the pitcher who is the most important. After all, it's the pitcher who puts the ball in play. It's the pitcher who is the team's offense.

Not only does the pitcher (along with his catcher) decide when to pitch the ball, but also how to pitch it. Should he deliver the ball high or low inside or outside? Should he pitch at top speed or something less? Should he make the ball curve or drop?

To be able to make the ball travel fast and change direction on the way to the plate, the pitcher is provided with a little hill called a "mound." Eighteen feet in diameter, the mound rises gradually to a maximum height of 10 inches above the level of the field.

At the center of the mound, there's a leveled-off area that

During the 1980s, Jack Morris of the Detroit Tigers was one of baseball's best pitchers. Here he tunes up before an exhibition game in 1988.

contains a white rubber slab called the pitcher's rubber. The rubber is 24 inches long and 6 inches wide. The front edge of the rubber is exactly 60 feet, 6 inches from the rear corner of home plate.

One rule concerning pitching says that the pitcher's back foot must remain in contact with the pitching rubber until he releases the ball. It's this rule that keeps the pitcher at the legal distance from the plate.

Another rule states that once the pitcher begins winding up he must continue the delivery to make it a legal pitch. If he fails to make the pitch after beginning his delivery, the umpire calls a balk. All base runners are permitted to advance one base. If the bases are empty, a ball is called.

A balk can also be called if the pitcher delivers a "quick pitch." The batter must be in a position to swing and be ready to hit; otherwise, the pitch doesn't count.

Still another rule, one in effect since 1920, makes it illegal for the pitcher to use any artificial means to make the ball do strange things. The pitcher cannot moisten the ball with spit or sweat or some form of grease, such as Vaseline. (It's even illegal for the pitcher to touch his mouth with his pitching hand while on the mound.) Nor is the pitcher permitted to cut or scuff the ball.

Gaylord Perry of the San Diego Padres and Don Sutton of the Los Angeles Dodgers were two pitchers often accused of applying spit to the ball. Perry, in fact, admitted to throwing spitters in a book he wrote at the tail end of his career.

When a pitcher, as the team's offense, is able to outwit and outperform the defense, he may become the game's winning pitcher. This is the pitcher on the winning team who is given credit in the official records for a victory.

To be credited with a win, a starting pitcher must pitch at least five complete innings. If the pitcher is replaced by a relief pitcher, his team must be leading at the time he is replaced for him to be eligible for the win.

To win twenty games in a season is every pitcher's goal. It means certain stardom.

The Strike Zone

The pitcher is required to throw the ball through an area above home plate called the strike zone. The strike zone is 17 inches wide, which is the width of home plate.

The lower limit of the strike zone is the top of the batter's

The width of home plate, the strike zone extends from the top of the knees to the uniform letters.

knees. For years, the upper limit of the strike zone was the batter's armpits. But baseball's Rules Committee changed the definition before the season of 1988. The new rule defined the upper level of the strike zone as the "midpoint between the top of the shoulder and the top of the uniform pants." By reducing the size of the strike zone, the rulesmakers were believed to be helping the pitcher.

While the rules define the strike zone in very precise terms, it is a somewhat flexible area. It varies to some degree according to the height of the batter. The taller the batter, the bigger the strike zone—naturally.

The size of the strike zone also varies with the degree of the batter's crouch. When Rickey Henderson bends deeply toward the plate as he takes his stance, he automatically shrinks the size of his strike zone. It is no wonder that Henderson is always among the league leaders in bases on balls.

The umpire is still another factor. The calling of strikes and balls is not an exact science. There are no visual guides such as foul lines or sidelines for the umpire to rely upon. Each call is a matter of judgment.

Balls and Strikes

The batter is allowed to swing at any delivery whether or not it enters the strike zone. But if the pitch passes through any portion of the strike zone, and the batter does not swing at it, the pitch is a "called" strike.

If a pitch misses the strike zone, and the batter does not swing at it, the pitcher is charged with a "ball."

On every trip to the plate, the batter is given three strikes and the pitcher is given four balls. If the pitcher throws four balls before the batter has had three strikes (or has hit a fair ball), the batter receives a base on balls (also known as a walk). When issued a base on balls, the batter is sent to first base automatically.

It's the bases on balls that force the pitcher to pitch the ball into the strike zone. Were he not afraid of issuing a walk, the pitcher would never have to throw the ball into the range of the batter's bat. The pitcher could pitch every pitch outside the batter's hitting range, hoping to get him to swing and miss.

Four balls figure into the strike count. Whenever a batter hits a foul ball, it is charged as a strike—unless the batter already has two strikes charged against him. In other words, a foul after two strikes doesn't count as anything (unless a fielder catches it on the fly, in which case it is an out). A batter can keep fouling off the ball without limit, remaining at bat until he swings and misses the third strike, "takes" a called third strike, or hits the ball into fair territory.

There is an exception, however. If the batter bunts the ball after two strikes, and it goes foul, it is strike three. The reason for this is easy to figure. When bunting, the batter has exceptional control of the ball. If he wanted, he could keep fouling off indefinitely, or until the pitcher wears himself out. To prevent this, a foul bunt is counted as a strike anytime it occurs.

A foul tip is another special case. A foul tip occurs when the ball caroms straight back off the bat and is caught by the catcher. A foul tip counts as a strike and the ball remains in play. When there are two strikes on the batter and a foul tip occurs, it's strike three and the batter is out.

The ball must be *caught*, however. If the catcher traps the ball, that is, catches it just after it rebounds, or catches it cleanly and then drops it, it is counted as a foul ball.

The Intentional Walk

Sometimes a pitcher walks a batter on purpose. This occurs when the pitcher wants to avoid pitching to a dangerous batter, with a weaker hitter next in the batting order.

You may also see an intentional base on balls when there are runners on second and third base, or merely on second, and first base is open. By walking the batter, a double play becomes much more of a possibility.

In either of the above situations, the pitcher throws four pitches very wide of the plate, well beyond the reach of the batter's bat. With the fourth pitch, the umpire signals the batter to take first base.

A batter can also get to first base because of interference on the part of the catcher. This occurs when the catcher touches the bat as the batter is swinging.

The Stretch Position

In winding up, the pitcher must keep his pivot foot (the left foot in the case of a right-handed pitcher) on the rubber. He swings his arms up over his head, steps toward the plate, whips the ball forward, and releases it.

When there is a runner on base, the pitcher has to cut short his windup. If the pitcher used a full windup, the runner would have the time needed to steal.

With a runner on base, the pitcher uses what is called a stretch motion. The pitcher lifts his hands to head level, then lowers them to a complete stop in a set position before delivering the ball (or throwing to the base).

The left-handed pitcher has an advantage in keeping the runner close to first. In the stretch position, the leftie faces first base; the right-hander faces third base. It's much easier for the left-hander to keep an eye on the runner and throw to first. The right-handed pitcher has to peer over his shoulder to eye the runner, and when throwing to first the rightie has to throw across his body.

The Pitches

While pitchers are forbidden to throw spitballs and several other types of pitches, there are plenty of others they can choose from. The pages that follow describe some of them.

Fastball—Sometimes called a smoker or a hummer, the

fastball is a pitch thrown at full speed. How fast does a fastball travel? The fastest ones are clocked at 97 to 98 miles an hour.

It's not hard to understand why a fastball is hard to hit, when you consider this statistic: A pitch traveling at "only" 90 miles an hour gets to the plate in less than half a second—in 0.42 seconds, to be exact.

Speed isn't the only factor. To be effective, a fastball must "move," that is, it must appear to "hop" or "rise" as it nears the batter.

Curveball—This is another bread-and-butter pitch. When thrown by a right-handed pitcher, the curve breaks away from the right-handed batter. A left-hander's curve breaks away from a left-handed hitter.

In throwing a curveball, the ball is gripped with the index finger and middle finger on the top or to the side. The thumb grips, too. A downward snap with the wrist and thumb at the time of release helps to give the ball its curving spin.

Doctors and trainers agree that Little Leaguers should not throw curveballs. Attempting to do so can damage the bones of a young person's arm and also stretch the liga-

With a runner on base, pitcher must lower hands to a complete stop before delivering the ball. John Candelaria of the Yankees is the pitcher here. Dan Gladden of the Twins is the runner, Don Mattingly, the first baseman.

ments in the elbow. A Little Leaguer who tries to develop a curveball can end up ruining his or her arm.

It's also possible to throw a curveball that breaks in the other direction—a reverse curve, known popularly as a screwball.

The screwball is released by snapping the wrist in the opposite direction of the curveball snap. This is very tough on one's arm, which is one reason only a few pitchers ever seek to master the screwball. In recent years, Fernando Valenzuela of the Los Angeles Dodgers was about the only pitcher who became a star by relying on this pitch.

Slider—The 1960s brought the widespread use of the slider, a pitch that is something between a fastball and a curve. It looks like a fastball until it gets three or four feet from the batter, then it breaks just enough to throw him off stride or miss the fat part of the bat.

The slider is popular for two reasons: it is easy for a pitcher to throw. But it is difficult for the batter to "read" or recognize.

In delivering a slider, the arm is held so the wrist is about halfway between the fastball and the curveball position. The pitch is thrown like a fastball, except that the pitcher flicks his wrist as he releases the ball, sort of as if he was turning a doorknob.

Despite the fact that the slider is very effective, pitchers are wary about using it because it can tear up a pitcher's arm. The Los Angeles Dodgers don't even want their coaches instructing their minor league pitchers how to throw it.

Knuckle Ball—Even harder to hit than the slider, the knuckle ball is a relatively slow pitch, traveling at 60 to 65 miles an hour, that breaks crazily as it nears home plate. Not even the pitcher knows exactly how it is going to break. Catchers have great difficulty trying to glove the pitch.

It is really not correct to call it a *knuckle ball*. The pitcher grips the ball, not with the knuckles, but with the tips of two fingers. When the ball is released, there is no snap. Instead, the wrist is pushed toward the batter. The result is that the ball has no spin, so it dips and dances on the way to the plate.

The knuckle-ball delivery is easy on the arm. Hoyt Wilhelm, a knuckleballer of the 1950s and 1960s, was still pitching in the major leagues at 49. The Niekro brothers, Phil and Joe, also kept pitching deep into their forties, thanks to the knuckler.

Why aren't there more knuckle-ball pitchers in the big leagues? Several reasons. First, major league scouts look for kids who can throw the ball really hard or have terrific breaking stuff. Second, it's hard for a knuckleballing youngster to find a kid catcher who can hold onto the pitch.

Last, it's not an easy pitch to learn. "You have to devote all of your time and attention to it," Phil Niekro once said. "You have to be willing to throw nothing but knucklers."

Sinker—This is a pitch that drops suddenly as it nears the plate—it "sinks."

The sinker is usually delivered with what is called a three-quarters release; that is, between an overhand and sidearm. The ball is gripped hard and thrown with a slight turn of the wrist.

Split-finger Fastball—This is the pitch of the 1980s, although many baseball people say that it is not really new. The split-finger is a very close relative of the forkball, a pitch that reliever Elroy Face used in 1959 to put together an 18-1 record.

The split-finger is squeezed between the pitcher's forefinger and middle finger, and pushed back, but not back so far it touches the webbing at the base of the fingers. (The forkball was held in much the same way, but tucked more deeply into the hand.)

The split-finger is thrown straight overhand—"over the top" as the pitchers say. The fastball is thrown in exactly the same way. But the split-finger doesn't act like a fastball.

Fastball is gripped firmly, fingers along the seams.

Curveball has to be
released with outward
twist and downward
snap.

Knuckle ball is
gripped with tips of
two fingers.

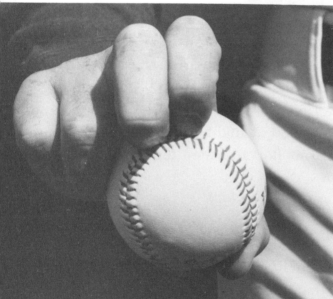

Split-finger delivery is
straight overhand.

It drops down as it nears the plate and breaks to the right or left.

Roger Craig, a pitching coach with the Tigers in 1974, taught the split-finger to the Detroit pitching staff. The Tigers won the World Series that year, thanks, at least in part to the split-finger.

A couple of seasons later, after Craig had become manager of the San Francisco Giants, he said that he believed that from 30 to 40 percent of pitchers in the National League were using the split-finger, or working on it.

But not every pitcher can pick it up. You have to have big hands and long fingers (which makes it as rare in Little League play as the 95-mile-an-hour fastball). Craig once told Roger Angell of *The New Yorker* that one pitcher he knew had even gone to bed at night with a ball strapped between his fingers in an effort to widen their grip.

Relief Pitchers

Baseball prides itself on its long history, the fact that it has been played for about a century and a half. Its roots go back much further than that. Nevertheless, baseball is changing all the time. One of the most dramatic changes in recent years concerns relief pitching.

While the game has always had pitchers whose job it was to rescue starters who get themselves in trouble, it's only in the past couple of decades that the relief pitcher has become so important. No team can hope to win today without a skilled bullpen crew.

During the early 1940s, relief pitchers were used in slightly more than one-half of all games. By the early 1960s, the figure had climbed to more than 70 percent of all games. Today, hardly a game is played in which a relief pitcher does not figure.

And not just one reliever is being used per game; often there are several of them. Besides the specialist who is expected to come into a contest in the eighth or ninth inning and put out the fire, we now have the "middle innings" reliever. He makes his appearance in the fourth or fifth inning and remains on the scene until the final stages.

This means that batters are constantly facing pitchers with fresh arms. And each has a different style and throws different kinds of pitches. There are no easy at-bats today.

Also, relief pitchers are much more skilled today than they used to be. The bullpen staff used to be made up of pitchers who were about ready to retire or simply were considered not good enough to start. Not any more. Nowadays relief pitchers are developed in the minor leagues. By the time they reach the major leagues, they're ready to become stars, and often they do. In recent years, Rich Gossage, who joined the Chicago Cubs in 1988 after four seasons with the San Diego Padres, and Dave Righetti of the New York Yankees have been the leaders, or at least among the leaders, in terms of numbers of saves.

A relief pitcher, instead of being credited with a save, can end up as the game's winning pitcher. This can occur when the starting pitcher has not pitched at least five

With forty saves in 1987, reliever Steve Bedrosian of Phillies captured Cy Young Award.

innings and is leading when replaced. Should the reliever then maintain the lead until the game ends, he gets the win.

A relief pitcher can also be credited with a win if his team assumes a lead that he maintains until the game ends. (If there is more than one relief pitcher in the game, the reliever judged by the official scorer to be the most effective is credited with the win.)

Umpires

Umpires play a vital role in each pitcher's life. Most major league games have four umpires. They are the first base umpire, second base umpire, third base umpire, and home plate umpire. The first and third base umpires not only rule on plays at their bases but also decide whether balls hit close to the foul lines are fair or foul.

During World Series play and in All-Star games, two additional umpires are used. They are stationed on the foul lines to help rule on balls hit down the lines.

The plate umpire is the game's umpire-in-chief. He is the final authority on the conduct of the game. It's the plate umpire who declares "Play Ball!" to start the game.

The home plate umpire performs a critical job. Every time the batter takes a pitch, the plate umpire must decide whether it is in or out of the strike zone, that is, whether the pitch is a strike or a ball.

The calling of balls and strikes is the most-used ruling in

all of sports. It occurs anywhere from 250 to 400 or more times during a game.

"Working the plate is the bread and butter of umpiring," American League umpire Joe Brinkman once told the *New York Times*. "If you can't do it well, you won't be an umpire."

Managers John McNamara of Red Sox and Tigers' Sparky Anderson meet with umpires before the game.

4

About Hitting

Many experts say that the act of hitting a pitched ball is the toughest thing to do in all of sports. A thrown baseball is like a missile, veering this way and that. The batter has about a half a second to decide the direction the ball is taking, whip the bat around and drive the ball into fair territory just out of the reach of the fielders.

As this suggests, hitting is kind of a reflex action, like putting out your hand when you're in danger of falling. But it is a trained reflex, a skill that's developed from many thousands of practice swings taken beginning with Little League days or before.

Despite the fact that successful hitting depends on one's ability to react fast, every good hitter follows certain rules. The hitter grips the bat firmly (but not tightly) and takes a comfortable stance. The shoulders and hips are level; the body's weight is on the balls of the feet.

Just before the ball leaves the pitcher's hand, the batter shifts his weight to his rear foot and cocks the bat a little farther over the shoulder. As the ball is released, the hitter strides forward with the front foot.

While young batters are taught to develop a level swing, many major league hitters actually hit down slightly on the ball. Hitting down results in hard smashes, balls that zip through the infield for base hits.

Power also comes from quick wrists. A good hitter can flick the bat into the ball in the blink of an eye. This gift enables the batter to wait until the last possible moment before swinging. The batter thus has more time to determine what kind of pitch is coming, and whether it is going to be high or low, inside or outside.

There's also a mental side to hitting. The hitter has to be patient and wait for a good pitch to hit.

What the hitter must beware of doing is swinging at a pitch that the pitcher wants him to swing at. Always trying to hit the pitcher's pitches is likely to get one a quick trip back to the minor leagues.

Some baseball experts claim that hitters today are better than ever. They have to be highly skilled in order to be able to cope with relief pitchers and the split-finger fastball and the other new pitches being thrown.

But today's hitters are aided by a new wave of hitting instructors, coaches whose chief task it is to work with young or troubled hitters. In days past, hitting instruction was a hit-or-miss business. It's as much a part of the modern game as tight-fitting uniforms.

Present-day base hitters also benefit from artificial grass.

They tailor their swings for the faster surfaces, learning to shell the ball right past the infielders.

Who are the best of the modern-day hitters? Any list must include the following:

• Wade Boggs of the Boston Red Sox, who, by the time he was twenty-eight, had won the league batting title three times.

• Don Mattingly of the New York Yankees won his first batting title as a rookie. Mattingly is said to be following in the tradition of Lou Gehrig and Joe DiMaggio, two of the New York team's all-time greats.

Right: Yankee first baseman Don Mattingly (right) is often hailed as one of baseball's best hitters—if not *the* best.

Left: Twins' Dan Gladden lines the ball for a single off John Candelaria of the Yankees.

• Tony Gwynn of the San Diego Padres, who averaged .325 for his first four seasons in the major leagues. Not only is Gwynn one of the best hitters in the game, he is also one of the outstanding defensive outfielders.

The list might also include Cal Ripkin of the Baltimore Orioles, Tim Raines of the Montreal Expos, and Jose Canseco of the Oakland A's.

But such hitters don't really worry good pitchers very much. They know how to handle them. "Don Mattingly is no big deal," says one. "You just walk him and pitch to the next guy."

Right-handers vs. Left-handers

There are advantages to being a left-handed hitter. One has to do with how fast the batter is able to get to first base. When the right-handed hitter hits the ball, he must check the momentum of his swing, turn his body and step across the plate as he starts for first base. But with the leftie, the momentum of his swing is in the direction of the base, and he is at least two steps closer to the base as he starts. These two steps are very critical when it comes to beating out infield hits.

Another reason that it's better to be a left-handed hitter is because most pitchers—about 75 percent of them—are right-handed. It is well known that left-handed hitters hit better against right-handed pitchers (and right-handed hitters do better against left-handed pitchers).

Why is this so? Imagine a right-handed hitter facing a left-handed pitcher. When the pitcher delivers, the ball comes from the first base side of the mound. The batter gets a clear view of it without having to turn his head.

The right-handed batter with a rightie on the mound has to turn his head to pick up the ball. This makes it harder for the hitter to figure out what the ball is going to do.

In addition, a left-handed hitter is likely to find it easier to hit a right-hander's curve ball. A "normal" curve tends to break away from the side from which it is thrown. A right-hander's curve breaks away from the right-hander hitter and toward the left-handed hitter, an advantage for the leftie.

When left-handed hitter swings, his stride is toward first base. This is Dave Bergman of the Tigers.

Bunting

Batters are also skilled in bunting—or should be. A batter bunts by turning to face the pitcher and holding the bat over the plate. The idea is to tap the ball a short distance into the infield.

There are two reasons for bunting. A batter may uncork a surprise bunt, hoping to catch the third baseman or first baseman off guard. That's bunting for a base hit.

More common is the sacrifice bunt, which usually takes place with a runner on first base or runners on first and second. The bunt is grabbed by the catcher, pitcher, or one of the infielders and the bunter is thrown out at first base. But the runners have moved up a base. The batter has "sacrificed" his turn at the plate for the sake of advancing the runners. A sacrifice bunt does not count as an official time at bat.

Neither does a sacrifice fly. This is a fly ball that enables a runner on third base to tag up and score.

The Batting Order

In running the team, the manager decides which players will play and decides the team's strategy. Another of the manager's daily tasks is making up the batting order. In so doing, the manager takes players with different kinds of hitting skills and tries to blend them in an explosive, run-producing force.

The batting order represents certain tried and proven theories. The lead-off man must be good at getting on base. The second batter has to be skilled at bunting and other techniques meant to advance the runner. The third batter is usually the best hitter on the team, the player with the highest batting average.

The fourth, fifth, and sixth batters supply the team's power; they drive in the runs. The fourth hitter, in fact, is sometimes called the "clean-up" hitter. With his powerful bat, the fourth batter is expected to "clean" the bases of runners.

As clean-up hitter, Toronto's George Bell won American League MVP award in 1987.

The seventh and eighth batters are seldom known for their hitting talent. They're more likely to be defensive specialists.

The ninth batter is traditionally the pitcher. In the American League, however, a designated hitter hits in place of the pitcher (see page 76). Nevertheless, the same theories apply when the batting order is being made out.

The opposing managers, or a coach or player who represents one or both of them, meet with the umpires at home plate before the game. The managers exchange copies of one another's batting order. A copy of each is also given to the umpire-in-chief.

During the game, the manager is likely to substitute frequently. The rules provide that a new player can be brought into the game at any time. The player replaced cannot return to the game. The new player takes the spot on the batting order of the player he replaced.

Most of baseball's substitutes are either relief pitchers or pinch-hitters. A pinch-hitter, called upon when a team is in serious need of hits and runs, is a player sent into the game in place of a weaker hitter.

5

Rules to Remember

A strikeout—covered in Chapter 3—is one of three basic ways of retiring a batter. Getting the batter to fly out or tagging the batter with the ball between bases are the other two.

A batter flies out after hitting a fair or foul ball that a fielder catches before it hits the ground.

Tagging a player out is a bit more complicated. In some cases, the fielder doesn't have to actually make a tag; the fielder can touch the base instead.

Suppose a fielder gloves a ground ball and throws it to the first baseman before the batter reaches first. The first baseman can tag the runner out.

But tag plays at first base could lead to dangerous collisions. After all, the batter is racing toward first at top speed and he usually arrives there at about the same time as the throw from the infielder. To avoid the meeting of bodies, the rulesmakers decided it would be all right for the first baseman, once he had the ball in his possession, to merely

Geronimo Berros pursues Lou Thornton in Toronto tagging drill.

touch the base with his foot. If he did that before the batter got to the base, the batter was out.

The basis of this ruling was that the batter, having hit the ball, was "forced" to run to first base. He *had* to try to reach the base safely. Getting the ball to the base before the runner arrived was enough to put the runner out.

This theory was extended to other bases and home plate. Suppose there is a runner on first and the batter hits the ball into fair territory. The runner on first base is "forced" to move to second base to open up first for the batter. So the rulesmakers decided it would be enough to touch second before the runner arrived there to put the runner out. This came to be known as a "force-out," or simply a "force."

One direct result of force plays is the double play. When, for instance, there is a runner on first and the batter hits a sharp grounder or bouncer, an infielder can rake in the ball and throw to second base for a force out. The infielder at second, after catching the ball and tagging the base, can rifle the ball to first base for a force-out there as well. That's two outs on one play, one of the most exciting plays in the game.

Sometimes an infielder makes a double play by himself, what is called an unassisted double play. Suppose there's a runner on first base. He takes a good-sized lead. The batter slams a line drive that is grabbed by the first baseman, who quickly steps on first base before the runner can get back. The first baseman has executed an unassisted double play.

There's also the triple play, a play in which three players are put out. Triple plays are rare, usually occurring only once or twice a season.

Especially rare are unassisted triple plays. There have been only eight in all of major league history. The first took place in 1909. The Cleveland Indians were playing the Boston Red Sox. Neal Ball of the Indians, playing short-stop, made a leaping catch of a line drive with runners on first base and second base. That was the first out. Ball stepped on second for the second out, then tagged the runner trapped between first and second for the third out.

There have been no unassisted triple plays since 1927. The last one was executed by Johnny Neun, a shortstop for the Detroit Tigers in a game against the Cleveland Indians on May 31 that year.

The Infield-fly Rule

Throughout baseball history, players have looked for and discovered loopholes in the rules, and tried to take advantage of them. Take the infield fly, for example.

Imagine this situation: Runners are on first and second base. There is one out. The batter hits a pop fly that can easily be caught by the second baseman. The runners hold their bases; they know they cannot advance until the ball is caught.

But the second baseman, poised to catch the ball, purposely lets it slip through his hands and drop at his feet. That means the runners are suddenly forced to run to the next base. They each have 90-feet to go—and the second baseman has the ball. It's an easy matter for the second baseman to tag the runner who is heading from first base to second and then to flip the ball to the first baseman to nab the hitter. It's a cinch double play.

Rulesmakers, in 1895, decided this play was unfair. They introduced the infield-fly rule.

In the situation described above, or one similar to it, the umpire signals "infield fly" as soon as he thinks that the ball can be caught by an infielder. The batter is automatically out. Even if an infielder lets the ball slip through his hands, the batter is still out. Knowing this, the runners react accordingly, each staying in contact with the base.

Running the Bases

Baseball rules display much common sense. Suppose a batter makes an out by hitting a fly ball. Before the ball is actually caught, there might be time for a runner to advance to the next base. But this would be a case of the runner benefitting through a failure on the part of the batter.

To prevent this, the rules say that when a ball is caught on the fly, the runner may not leave the base occupied until the ball has touched the fielder's glove. If the runner does leave the base, the fielder can throw the ball there. If the ball arrives before the runner gets back, the runner is out.

Sometimes the runner, believing the ball will not be caught, takes off for the next base. But the fielder makes a miracle catch. The runner then has to make a desperate attempt to return to the base. If the runner fails to do so, a double play results.

There is a way, however, that runners can advance on fly-ball outs. They do so by "tagging up." Suppose there is a runner on third base (and fewer than two outs). The batter drives a fly ball deep to the outfield. The runner, realizing the ball is going to be caught, returns to the base. But as soon as the outfielder touches the ball, the runner streaks

Vince Coleman of the Cardinals unlimbers baseball's fastest legs.

for home plate, seeking to beat the outfielder's throw. Critical runs are often scored by means of tag-up plays.

Runners can also advance on ground-outs. Let's say there's one out and a runner on second when a ground ball is hit to the second baseman. The runner breaks for third almost at the crack of the bat. The second baseman, after scooping up the ball, tosses it to first base. It's a sure out. However, the runner ends up on third.

There's still another way base runners can advance—by stealing. A steal occurs when a runner breaks for and reaches the next base safely, before the opposing team can get the ball to a defensive player to make a tag. (The runner has to be tagged; he is not "forced" to go to the next base on a steal.)

Stealing is an art. A good base stealer has to be very fast—naturally. But speed is only part of it.

Other key factors are getting a big lead, starting fast and knowing exactly the right moment to take off. As this suggests, the runner must know the pitcher and the motion the pitcher uses.

Boston's Todd Benzinger guards the base against Scott Lusader of the Tigers, a potential thief.

The runner has to know when the pitcher intends to throw to first base and when the pitcher is merely bluffing a throw. The runner also has to be able to detect when the pitcher has reached the point of no return in his windup and delivery, when he *has* to throw to the plate.

In addition, the runner has to get the right type of pitch. Trying to steal on a fastball makes it difficult. A curve, or any breaking pitch, is better. It takes longer for a breaking pitch to get to the catcher.

The catcher, of course, plays a key role. He guns the ball to the infielder at the base.

Even so, it's a well-known fact that the runner steals "on the pitcher," not "on the catcher."

In the American League, Yankees' Rickey Henderson is often No. 1 base stealer.

6

Major Leagues, Minor Leagues

The baseball season lasts a bit more than eight months—from mid-February to late October. It begins during the first or second week of February when empty tractor-trailers appear outside the locker rooms of the 26 major league ball parks. Clubhouse personnel and groundskeepers spend the day loading the trucks with baseball gear. At nightfall, the loaded trucks head for each team's training camp. There are eight camps in Arizona and eighteen in Florida.

The cargo loaded into each truck is pretty much the same. In the case of the New York Yankees, it includes 27 trunks of baseball gear, 200 uniforms, 200 bats, stacks of medical supplies, three exercise bikes, two pitching machines, and 60 boxes of dark blue Yankee jackets to be sold as souvenirs at the concession stands.

A few days later, the trailers arrive at the training camps and everything is unloaded.

There are two reasons for spring training: to get players

Outside Yankee Stadium, baseball gear is loaded aboard a huge tractor-trailer for trip south to spring training camp.

in condition for the season and to inspect young players who may be ready to play in the major leagues.

During the first couple of weeks, players work on fundamentals—fielding, throwing, running, hitting, sliding, and bunting.

After a few days, the manager organizes the players into teams that play one another. Games seem friendly and easygoing. But the manager and coaches are keeping a close eye on each player.

After a couple of weeks, each team begins playing exhibition games, scheduling teams for both leagues. Everything is more serious. While games do not count in the standings, they're very important to rookie players and veterans alike. Jobs are won and lost on the basis of how players perform.

In mid-March, there's the first "cutdown date." The manager and his staff trim ten or twelve players from the squad. Some of these players are assigned to minor league teams. Others are released, which means that their chance

to become major leaguers has slipped away. Cutdown day is gloomy.

During the last week in March, more players are cut or traded. Some of the older players who are released know that their careers are over. They say their good-byes and leave quickly.

On the final day of camp, a tractor-trailer truck appears outside the camp headquarters. Into it are loaded the team's equipment. The truck heads for the home ball park. Spring training is over. Players board the team plane for the flight home or to the ball park where the club is scheduled for Opening Day. The long season lies ahead.

Philadelphia Phillies loosen up at their spring training camp at Clearwater, Florida.

The Regular Season

Each of the 26 major league teams plays 162 games during the regular season. Half of a team's games are played at its home park and half in the parks of opponents.

Oddly, American League baseball is a little bit different than baseball played in the National League. American League teams use a tenth player, a designated hitter.

The designated hitter, or dh, for short, bats in the place of the pitcher. He does not hold down a position in the field. When his team's turn at bat is over and his teammates hurry out onto the field to take up their defensive positions, the designated hitter remains on the bench. The American League adopted the designated hitter rule in 1973.

In each major league, teams are divided into an Eastern and Western Division. The team that finishes the season with the best record in its division wins the division championship.

The champion of the Eastern Division then meets the champion of the Western Division in a league playoff. The first team to win four playoff games becomes the league champion.

The two league champions meet in the World Series. The first team to win four games in Series play is the world champion.

Baseball has followed this format since 1969, the year of the first playoff games. The Atlanta Braves and Minnesota

MAJOR LEAGUE BASEBALL TEAMS

American League

Eastern Division   *Western Division*
Baltimore Orioles   California Angels
Boston Red Sox   Chicago White Sox
Cleveland Indians   Kansas City Royals
Detroit Tigers   Minnesota Twins
Milwaukee Brewers   Oakland Athletics
New York Yankees   Seattle Mariners
Toronto Blue Jays   Texas Rangers

National League

Eastern Division   *Western Division*
Chicago Cubs   Atlanta Braves
Montreal Expos   Cincinnati Reds
New York Mets   Houston Astros
Philadelphia Phillies   Los Angeles Dodgers
Pittsburgh Pirates   San Diego Padres
St. Louis Cardinals   San Francisco Giants

Twins were baseball's first playoff winners. (The 1969 New York Mets and Baltimore Orioles were the first losing playoff teams.)

The World Series, of course, is much older. The first World Series was played in 1903. The American League's Boston Pilgrims defeated the National League champion Pittsburgh Pirates.

The next year, 1904, the Pilgrims won the American League title again. The powerful New York Giants won in

Jubilant New York Met fans hail catcher Gary Carter at victory parade following team's World Series win in 1986.

the National League. But there was no World Series. The Giants refused to play; the proud New Yorkers were afraid of being embarrassed by the Pilgrims.

But that never happened again. The World Series was played in 1905, and has been played every year since.

The All-Star Game

The All-Star game is another exciting event on the baseball calendar. It matches the season's American League stars against the outstanding players in the National

League. Fans, by voting, choose the two starting lineups, except for the pitchers. The teams' managers choose the starting pitchers and substitutes. The managers of the All-Star teams, incidentally, are the World Series managers from the previous year.

The first All-Star game dates to July 6, 1933. It was played at Chicago's Comiskey Park. The American League won, 4-2, helped by Babe Ruth's two-run homer.

The All-Star game was cancelled in 1945 because of World War II. Night baseball was introduced to All-Star play in 1967, when the game was played at Anaheim Stadium, Anaheim, California.

The American League showed itself to be superior to the National League in the early years of the All-Star game, winning 12 of the first 16 contests. But during the 1970s and 1980s, the National League dominated.

Honoring Players

Once the World Series is over and before spring training begins the following year, hardly a week passes without one player or another being hailed for batting or fielding excellence. Here are some of the awards that players receive.

MVP—The outstanding performer in each league each year wins the Most Valuable Player award. Since 1931, MVP's have been chosen by the Baseball Writers of America.

NATIONAL LEAGUE STADIUMS

Team	Stadium	Type of Grass Surface	Seating Capacity
Atlanta Braves	Atlanta-Fulton County Stadium	Natural	52,006
Chicago Cubs	Wrigley Field	Natural	38,040
Cincinnati Reds	Riverfront Stadium	Artificial	52,392
Houston Astros	Astrodome	Artificial	45,000
Los Angeles Dodgers	Dodger Stadium	Natural	56,000
Montreal Expos	Olympic Stadium	Artificial	59,149
New York Mets	Shea Stadium	Natural	55,601
Philadelphia Phillies	Veterans Stadium	Artificial	66,271
Pittsburgh Pirates	Three Rivers Stadium	Artificial	54,438
St. Louis Cardinals	Busch Stadium	Artificial	50,222
San Diego Padres	Jack Murphy Stadium	Natural	58,433
San Francisco Giants	Candlestick Park	Natural	58,000

The American League was the first to choose a MVP, when, in 1922, a special committee selected George Sisler of the St. Louis Browns for the honor.

In 1924, another special committee selected the National League's first MVP—Dazzy Vance of the Brooklyn Dodgers.

Trivia question: Who is the only player to be selected as an MVP in both leagues?

Answer: Frank Robinson. He was the National League MVP in 1961 as a member of the Cincinnati Reds, and the

American League MVP in 1966 when he played for the Baltimore Orioles.

Cy Young Award—Each year the outstanding pitcher in each of the major leagues, as determined by the Baseball Writers Association of America, receives the Cy Young Award. The award is named in honor of the legendary Denton True (Cy) Young. From 1889 through 1911, Young,

AMERICAN LEAGUE STADIUMS

Team	Stadium	Type of Grass Surface	Seating Capacity
Baltimore Orioles	Memorial Stadium	Natural	54,076
Boston Red Sox	Fenway Park	Natural	33,583
California Angels	Anaheim Stadium	Natural	64,573
Chicago White Sox	Comiskey Park	Natural	44,087
Cleveland Indians	Cleveland Stadium	Natural	74,208
Detroit Tigers	Tiger Stadium	Natural	52,806
Kansas City Royals	Royals Stadium	Artificial	40,625
Milwaukee Brewers	Milwaukee County Stadium	Natural	53,192
Minnesota Twins	Hubert H. Humphrey Metrodome	Artificial	55,244
New York Yankees	Yankee Stadium	Natural	57,545
Oakland A's	Oakland Coliseum	Natural	50,219
Seattle Mariners	Kingdome	Artificial	59,438
Texas Rangers	Arlington Stadium	Natural	43,508
Toronto Blue Jays	Exhibition Stadium	Artificial	43,737

Mike Schmidt of the Phillies was three-time winner of National League's MVP award.

pitching for the Cleveland Spiders, St. Louis Cardinals, and Boston Pilgrims, won 511 games, the all-time record.

When the Cy Young Award was established in 1956, it was given to the standout pitcher in the major leagues. Don Newcombe of the Dodgers won the award that year. Since 1967, two awards have been given annually, one to a pitcher in each league.

Gold Glove Award—To salute excellence in fielding, Rawlings Sporting Goods established the Gold Glove

Award in 1957. A handsome trophy goes to the outstanding fielder at each position, as voted by members of the Baseball Writers Association of America.

Rookie-of-the-Year Award—The outstanding first year player in each league receives the Rookie-of-the-Year Award. Players are chosen by members of the Baseball Writers Association of America on the basis of all-around performance.

Dodgers' Don Newcombe, the first player to win Cy Young Award.

The National League gave the first Rookie-of-the-Year Award in 1947. Jackie Robinson of the Brooklyn Dodgers was the winner. The American League followed in 1949, with Roy Sievers of the St. Louis Browns capturing the prize.

Triple Crown—The Triple Crown is one of the rarest accomplishments in baseball. To win the Triple Crown, one must lead the league for the season in three categories: batting average, runs batted in, and home runs.

Only nine players have been Triple Crown winners. Carl Yastrzemski of the Boston Red Sox won the Triple Crown in 1967, and no player has won it since.

Hall of Fame—Baseball's all-time greats are honored by being named members of Baseball's Hall of Fame. Since 1936, when the first five players were inducted, more than two hundred others have been chosen for membership.

The Hall of Fame itself is located in Cooperstown, New York. It occupies a separate wing of the National Baseball Museum and Hall of Fame. A plaque for each of the honored players is displayed in the Hall of Fame gallery.

New members are elected to the Hall of Fame each year by the Baseball Writers of America. In order to be eligible for membership, a player must be retired for at least five

Lou Gehrig of the Yankees (left) won the Triple Crown in 1934. Jimmy Foxx of the Athletics (center) won it in 1933. But the prize eluded home-run hero Babe Ruth.

years and have played in the major leagues for at least ten years. The player must receive votes from at least 75 percent of those voting.

The Hall of Fame Committee on Baseball Veterans also selects players. Sometimes these are black players who were active in the Negro leagues before 1947, the year that black players were first able to play in the major leagues.

Satchel Paige, who regularly recorded 40 victories a season in black leagues, was elected to Hall of Fame in 1971.

Minor Leagues

It's in the minor leagues that most players receive the training needed to enable them to play baseball on a major league level. There are fewer minor leagues today than there used to be, but during the 1980s, minor league baseball—the bush leagues—enjoyed a period of tremendous growth.

In 1987, there were seventeen minor leagues with 144 teams. The leagues are divided into three classifications—Class AAA (the highest league level), Class AA, and Class A.

There are also Rookie Leagues, which are the lowest rung of the ladder. Most Rookie Leagues contain players right out of college or even high school.

Each of the 26 major league teams must support at least four minor league teams. But some major league clubs have as many as six or more.

When a major league team supports a minor league team, it pays the salaries of the players and coaches, and provides uniforms and equipment.

In recent years, attendance at minor league games has soared. In fact, in 1987, minor league attendance topped 20 million for the first time since 1934.

Minor league baseball is enjoying newfound popularity partly because teams have begun to promote themselves vigorously. They bring in musical groups for concerts and schedule old-timers' games with retired major league players.

When a player signs his first professional contract with a major league team, the player becomes the property of that team. The team may assign a newly signed player to a Rookie League. As the player's ability improves, he moves up the minor league ladder.

If he continues to show improvement, the player may sign a major league contract. This means he becomes one of the forty players over which the major league teams have direct control.

The player can still be sent back to the minors. In fact, he can be sent back three times. But after the third time, he can't be sent back again unless he is first offered to other major league teams.

Amateur Leagues

The major leagues and minor leagues offer baseball to watch. They're more for the fan than the player.

But when it comes to playing baseball, people turn to nonprofessional leagues. Teenagers play baseball in Babe Ruth leagues and American Legion leagues. High schools and colleges offer competition. The National Baseball Congress sponsors amateur leagues for adults.

For younger players, there's Little League Baseball. Little League competition involves more than two million boys and girls. In fact, no sports program in the world is bigger than Little League Baseball.

Little League Baseball—Major league rules call for 90 feet between bases and a distance of 60 feet, 6 inches from the pitcher's rubber to home plate. At the foul lines, outfield distances are around 325 feet. In Little League play, the distance between bases is 60 feet and the pitching distance is 46 feet. Outfield distances of 200 feet are recommended.

Little League Baseball got started in Williamsport, Pennsylvania, in 1939. At first, the program was offered only to 8-to-12-year-old boys. Today, the program includes girls and older boys. For 13-to-15 year-olds, there's Senior League competition, and there's Big League play for 16-to-18-year-olds. The Senior Leagues and Big Leagues play on a regular-size diamond.

Baseball as played in Little Leagues is very similar to the game that is played on a big league level. But there are important differences in the way Little League and major league baseball are structured.

The biggest difference has to do with leagues. In Little League play, the league is the basic unit. It is usually made up of from 8 to 10 teams.

More than 14,000 Little Leagues operate each season. Major league baseball, of course, has only two leagues. Each is divided into divisions. The division champions play in the World Series.

At age of 12, Nicole Levesque, from South Shaftsbury, Vermont, helped to pioneer girls' participation in Little Leagues.

To decide the Little League world champions, each Little League is first encouraged to choose the best players from several teams. These players make up an all-star team. It's this team that represents the league and goes on to play all-star teams from other leagues to decide the regional, national, and then world title.

Another difference between Little League and the big leagues has to do with the home playing field. In the major leagues, each team has its own home diamond. But in Little League competition, all the teams in a league use the same diamond.

One curious fact about Little League play in recent years is that the world championsip has usually been won by a team from Asia. In fact, when Hua Lin, Taiwan, beat Irvine, California, 21-1, in the 1987 Little League World Series, it marked the seventeenth series victory for a team from the Far East in twenty-one years.

Other Leagues—The American Legion, an organization made up of veterans of the United States armed forces, sponsors nationwide baseball competition for 15-to-18-year-olds. It involves an annual world series tournament for the American Legion's eight regional champions.

Many thousands of other youngsters in cities throughout the United States and Canada take part in Babe Ruth Baseball. Founded in 1951, the Babe Ruth program offers competition for youngsters ages 9 through 12, 13 through 15, and 16 through 18.

7

Looking Back

Baseball developed from the sport of rounders, which was played in England in the 1600s. In rounders, the idea was to hit a ball with a bat and advance around three bases. Each base was stake-driven into the ground.

Fielders put out base runners, not by tagging them, but by trying to hit them with a thrown ball. This was known as "plugging" the runner.

When English settlers arrived in what is now Massachusetts in the early 1600s, they brought not only their system of government and certain religious beliefs with them, they also brought their social customs. One was rounders.

By the early 1700s, many variations of rounders were being played. Different names were used for these games, including one old cat, two old cat, and, simply, town ball. In one old cat, only one base was used, and the game required only three players, a pitcher, catcher, and batter.

With more players and another base, the game became two old cat.

The *Little Pretty Pocket Book* is evidence that baseball is well over two hundred years old. This book, published in 1767, offers a picture of boys playing a game with bases arranged in a diamond shape. Beneath the picture, there's a poem titled "Base Ball." It reads:

> The ball once struck off,
>   Away flies the boy
> To the next destined point,
>   And then home with joy.

In other words, boys were batting the ball, running from one point to another and scoring runs as early as 1767.

In time, the three posts or stakes were replaced with flat stones and then with sacks filled with sand. Instead of throwing the ball at the runner to get an out, fielders began tagging runners, as they do today.

In spite of the evidence that baseball grew out of the

game of rounders, some people believe that a young man named Abner Doubleday created the game of baseball in the small village in central New York State called Cooperstown. (The Baseball Hall of Fame and Museum is located in Cooperstown.) This story, which is about eighty years old, is known to have little truth to it. Doubleday, who grew up to become a general in the United States army, may have helped to make baseball popular in central New York, but he never "invented" the game.

Baseball Gets a Rulebook

Alexander J. Cartwright rightfully holds the title of "father of organized baseball." Cartwright, from New York City, played the game with his friends in the early 1840s. In 1845, Cartwright founded a team called the Knickerbocker Base Ball Club of New York. At the same time, Cartwright wrote a set of rules for the game. These set the distance between bases at 90 feet, provided for nine players on a side, and established the difference between fair and foul territory.

On June 19, 1846, Cartwright's Knickerbocker Club and another team, the New York Nine, took a ferryboat across the Hudson River to Hoboken, New Jersey. There, at Elysian Fields, they played what historians now call the first baseball game. The New York Nine won, 23-1.

The Civil War, which raged from 1861–1865, helped to spread baseball far and wide. Union soldiers who had

There have been many changes in baseball since the late 1800s, but the essentials have remained the same.

played the game in their hometowns, continued to play it in army camps and, when captured, in prison stockades. Other soldiers learned the game from them. After the war, soldiers who had learned the game returned home and taught it to their friends.

A convention of baseball teams held in New York in 1866 drew representatives from more than 100 clubs. The next year, 1867, 237 clubs were represented at the convention, some from as far away as Indiana, Illinois, and Wisconsin.

Beginnings of the Pro Game

All of these teams were amateur teams. The players were not paid. In 1869, a team called the Cincinnati Red Stockings decided to pay its players. Harry Wright, the team's captain and star center fielder, earned $1,200, a good salary in those days. The Red Stockings went on a national tour, playing every well-known baseball team between Massachusetts and California. They won 65 games and tied one. The tie occurred when the Haymakers of Troy, New York, walked off the field in the sixth inning because of an argument about a foul tip. The score was 17-17 at the time.

On their tour, the Red Stockings traveled 11,877 miles and played before 200,000 people. When they returned to Cincinnati, a victory banquet was held in their honor. At the banquet, the club president declared, "I'd rather be president of the Cincinnati Red Stockings than president of the United States!"

The success of the Red Stockings led other teams to form professional teams. The next step was to organize teams into leagues.

Early in 1876, a group of businessmen and club owners, led by William Hulbert, owner of the Chicago White Stockings, formed the National League. On April 22, 1876, the first National League game, Boston vs. Philadelphia at

Philadelphia, was played. Boston defeated the home team, 6-5, before 3,000 fans.

The National League remained baseball's only successful league until 1901. That year the American League was organized.

In 1900, the National League had teams in these cities: Boston, Brooklyn, Chicago, Cincinnati, New York City, Philadelphia, Pittsburgh, and St. Louis. In 1903, two years after its founding, the American League represented teams in Boston, Chicago, Cleveland, Detroit, New York City, Philadelphia, St. Louis, and Washington, D.C.

From these beginnings, baseball mushroomed in popularity. No other sport could offer such colorful players or dramatic moments. Baseball became known as America's "national pastime."

The First Commissioner

Baseball's history has not been made up of one sun-filled day after another. There have been some clouds and storms. Take, for example, what happened in 1919, the year the Cincinnati Reds surprised the baseball world by upsetting the Chicago White Sox in the World Series.

The next year, 1920, eight White Sox players were accused of "throwing" the Series. Bribed by gamblers, it was said they had lost on purpose. The scandal rocked baseball.

The owners responded by hiring a Commissioner of Baseball, someone to rule over the game. The man the owners chose was Kenesaw Mountain Landis, a federal judge.

Landis banned the players involved in the World Series scandal from playing baseball for life. His action helped to restore public confidence in the game.

Gambling scandal rocked baseball in 1920.

The year 1920 is also important because it was when Babe Ruth was traded by the Boston Red Sox to the New York Yankees. In the seasons that followed, Ruth and his booming bat would write one of the most exciting chapters in baseball history.

Before Ruth, no player had ever hit more than 24 home runs in a season. In 1920, Ruth slammed an amazing 54 home runs. He hit more than 50 homers in four seasons, including a record 60 in 1927. His career record of 714 homers lasted almost forty years.

Ruth's name was in the headlines frequently. He opened Yankee Stadium with a home run against the Boston Red Sox. On several occasions, he made bedside visits to sick children, promised to hit a home run for them—and did. At the age of forty, he wound up his career by smacking three home runs in a game at Forbes Field in Pittsburgh.

Fans flocked to the ball parks to see Babe Ruth. And other players started imitating him by swinging for the fences. Home runs became an important part of the game.

Baseball Goes Electronic

The development of radio and, later, television helped spread the popularity of baseball. The first radio broadcast took place on August 25, 1921, when station KDKA in Pittsburgh transmitted a play-by-play account of a game between the Pirates and the Philadelphia Phillies. Soon after, the radio networks began covering the World Series

and other important contests. People in places that did not have major league teams could now follow the sport.

Baseball made its first appearance on television on August 26, 1939, over station W2XBS. Many teams began televising their games in the late 1940s and early 1950s.

Breaking Barriers

The most important happening in modern baseball took place in 1947. That's the year that Jackie Robinson opened the season at second base for the Brooklyn Dodgers. Robinson was black. He was the first black player to play in the major leagues.

Before 1947, baseball was segregated. Black players played in leagues made up almost entirely of blacks. They were called Negro leagues.

Negro leagues developed their own stars whose skills rivaled those of Babe Ruth, Ty Cobb, and other major league greats. But stars of the Negro leagues seldom saw their names in the daily newspapers. They played almost in secrecy, known only to black fans. These stars included Satchel Paige, Cool Papa Bell, and Josh Gibson. These three, along with several other black stars, are now members of baseball's Hall of Fame.

Other trailblazers among blacks include Jim Gilliam of the Los Angeles Dodgers, who became the first black

Colorful Babe Ruth triggered a baseball boom.

Jackie Robinson, baseball's first major league black player.

coach in 1965; Emmett Ashford, the first black umpire (1966); Frank Robinson of the Cleveland Indians, the first black manager (1975); and Bill Lucas of the Atlanta Braves, the first black general manager (1977).

At the same time black players began entering the major leagues, the sport started shifting franchises and expanding. As a result, major league baseball was introduced to the West Coast, the South, the Southwest, and Canada.

Breaking Records

Recent years have seen some of baseball's most noted records fall. In 1961, Roger Maris, an outfielder for the

A ticket to a "colored" All-Star game in 1941.

Yankees, hit 61 home runs, topping Babe Ruth's record. Lou Brock, an outfielder for the St. Louis Cardinals, set a career record for stolen bases. Brock's total stood at 938 when he retired in 1979. The record of 892 steals had been held by Ty Cobb.

On April 8, 1974, Hank Aaron of the Atlanta Braves hit his 715th home run, breaking another of Ruth's records. Aaron, now an executive with the Braves, ended his playing career in 1976 with 755 home runs. That's a record that seems unbreakable. But so did Ruth's.

On September 11, 1981, Pete Rose of the Cincinnati Reds, broke Ty Cobb's record of 4,191 major league hits. Rose, who went on to manage the Reds, made his last

---

FRANCHISE SHIFTS AND ADDITIONS

National League

1953   The Boston Braves become the Milwaukee Braves.

1958   The Brooklyn Dodgers become the Los Angeles Dodgers; the New York Giants become the San Francisco Giants.

1962   The National League expands to ten teams, adding the New York Mets and the Houston Colt 45's. (The Colt 45's later become the Houston Astros.)

1966   The Milwaukee Braves become the Atlanta Braves.

1969   The National League expands to twelve teams, adding the Montreal Expos and San Diego Padres.

FRANCHISE SHIFTS AND ADDITIONS

American League

1954   The St. Louis Browns become the Baltimore Orioles.

1955   The Philadelphia Athletics become the Kansas City Athletics.

1961   The Washington Senators become the Minnesota Twins.

1962   The American League expands to ten teams, adding the Los Angeles Angels (later to become the California Angels) and the Washington Senators (to replace the former Washington Club).

1969   The Kansas City Athletics become the Oakland Athletics.

1970   The American League expands to twelve teams, adding the Kansas City Royals and Seattle Pilots.

1970   The Seattle Pilots become the Milwaukee Brewers.

1972   The Washington Senators become the Texas Rangers.

1977   The American League expands to fourteen teams, adding the Toronto Blue Jays and Seattle Mariners.

appearance as a hitter on August 17, 1986 (and struck out). By that time, he had accumulated 4,256 hits.

There have been enormous changes in baseball since the early 1900s. Players used to earn about the same amount of money as bus drivers or postal clerks. That's changed. In the late 1980s, the average salary in the major leagues was close to half a million dollars. Dan Quisenberry, a relief

Now an executive with the Atlanta Braves, Hank Aaron, with 755 homers, holds all-time record.

pitcher for the Kansas City Royals, received a salary of $2,292,509 in 1987.

Modern-day baseball means artificial turf and automatic tarps for covering the infields when it rains. There are ballgirls and ballboys and, in some parks, fireworks after home runs. There are dancing-waters displays in the outfields and escalators to whisk fans to their seats.

But some things have not changed. There are three strikes and you're out, nine innings to a game, and the team that bags the most runs wins. There are two big leagues, two summer-long pennant races, and the World Series in October to decide the championship. These are things worth keeping.

Figuring Averages

In baseball, unlike most other sports, players' performances are always being graded. It's like getting a report card but getting it every day of the week, Saturdays and Sundays included. And instead of being sent to one's parents or guardian, the information is published in the daily newspapers.

In the case of batters, this report is called a batting average. With fielders, it's a fielding average. Pitchers, relievers as well as starters, get two grades. One is called the won-lost percentage; the other is an earned-run average.

Let's look at these one by one.

A player's skill as a hitter is expressed by his batting average, which is abbreviated BA or, simply, Avg.

To figure a batting average, divide the number of at-bats into the number of hits. Carry the result out to three decimal places.

Suppose a batter came to the plate 10 times and got 3 hits. That's a .300 batting average, figured like this:

$$
10\,\overline{\smash{\big)}\,3.000} \atop {}
$$

```
        .300
10 √ 3.000
      3 0
      0 0
```

Let's take another example. Suppose a batter goes to the plate 483 times. He gets 162 hits. That figures out to a .334 batting average, calculated like this:

```
          .335
483 √ 162.000
      144 9
       17 10
       14 49
        2 610
        2 415
          195
```

Keep in mind, however, that not every trip to the plate is an "official" time at bat. To be counted as an official time at bat, the batter must be given an opportunity to hit. Thus, when a batter is issued a base on balls, it is not an official time at bat. Nor is an at-bat recorded when the batter is hit by a pitch, advances a runner by means of a bunt (called a sacrifice hit), hits a fly ball that enables a runner to tag up (a sacrifice fly), or is awarded first base because of the interference of the catcher.

A "hit" is any ball struck by the batter that enables him to reach base safely without an error by a fielder. Each single, double, triple, and home run counts as one hit in figuring a batting average.

A batting average of .300 or higher for a season is excellent (similar to an A on one's report card). An average of .400 is phenomenal, something like getting a school merit award.

Since the year 1900, only eight major league players have hit .400 or higher. The list includes Ty Cobb of the Detroit Tigers and Rogers Hornsby of the St. Louis Cardinals, each of whom did it three times.

Ted Williams, with a .406 average (456 at-bats, 185 hits) in 1941, was the last player in the major leagues to hit .400.

Another important statistic for a hitter is the number of runs batted in—RBIs. Whenever a run scores as a result of a batter's hit, the batter is credited with a run batted in. If the batter should clout a home run, he automatically gets one run batted in for the homer. He also gets an RBI for however many runners happened to be on base.

A batter also gets credit for a run batted in whenever he walks with the bases full, which forces in a run. Last, any time a run scores as a direct result of an out made by the batter, the batter gets credit for an RBI. This usually occurs on a long fly or a ground-out that brings in a runner from third base.

Fielding Averages

A fielder's average is figured in much the same way as a batting average. It expresses a player's efficiency as a

Ted Williams (left) of the Boston Red Sox (here with Joe
DiMaggio), with a .406 average in 1941, was the last major
leaguer to bat .400 or better.

fielder. In major league play, fielders' averages are always well above .950.

In figuring a fielding average, the first step is to determine the total chances for the player. A "chance" is the

Each season, 18 players, nine in each league, win this award for fielding excellence.

opportunity to put out a runner by either fielding a batted ball or making a play on a base runner. *Total* chances is the sum of all putouts, assists, and errors. (These are explained in the section of this book titled "Baseball Words and Terms.")

Divide the number of total chances into the sum of putouts and assists. Carry the result to three decimal places.

A player who accepts 1,000 total chances (putouts plus assists) over a season and makes only 10 errors, has a .990 fielding average.

$$
\begin{array}{r}
.990 \\
1{,}000 \overline{\smash{)}990.000} \\
\underline{990\ 0} \\
000\ 0
\end{array}
$$

Here's another example; it concerns a player with 1,121 putouts and 66 assists, for 1,195 total chances. He made 8 errors.

$$
\begin{array}{r}
.993 \\
1195 \overline{\smash{)}1187.000} \\
\underline{1075\ 5} \\
111\ 50 \\
\underline{107\ 55} \\
3\ 950 \\
\underline{3\ 585} \\
365
\end{array}
$$

Naturally, a fielder who has made no errors has a fielding average of 1,000.

Pitching Statistics

A pitcher's won-lost percentage is easy to figure. Simply divide the total number of games pitched (wins plus losses) into the total number of victories. Carry the result out to three decimal places. Here's an example:

Total wins: 19
Total losses: 5
Total games: 24

```
              .7916
24 √ 19.0000
      16 8
       2 20
       2 16
         40
         24
         16
```

Rounded off to three decimal places, the percentage is .792.

While a won-lost percentage gives some insight into a pitcher's ability over a given period of time, most baseball observers prefer to grade pitchers on the basis of their earned run averages. This is a statistic that reports the average number of earned runs allowed by the pitcher every nine innings.

To find a pitcher's ERA or earned run average, you first divide the total number of earned runs given up by the total number of innings pitched. You then multiply the result by nine.

What is an "earned run" anyhow? It is a run scored

Bob Gibson's 1.12 ERA in 1968 is the lowest in baseball history.

before the third putout of the inning and for which the pitcher is responsible.

If an error or a passed ball contributes to the scoring of a run, which would not have scored otherwise, it is an "unearned run." The pitcher is not held responsible for unearned runs.

Here is an example, based on 76 earned runs allowed in 175 innings of pitching.

$$
\begin{array}{r}
.434 \\
175\overline{)76.000} \\
70\ 0 \\
\hline
6\ 00 \\
5\ 25 \\
\hline
750 \\
700 \\
\hline
50
\end{array}
$$

The result—.434—is the number of earned runs allowed per inning expressed as a percentage. That figure must be multiplied by 9.

$$
\begin{array}{r}
.434 \\
\times\ 9 \\
\hline
3.906
\end{array}
$$

Earned run averages are expressed to two decimal places. In the above example, the ERA is 3.91.

An earned run average of less than 4.00 is considered very good. An ERA of less than 3.00 is exceptional. The lowest ERA in major league history for a season is 1.12, recorded by Bob Gibson of the St. Louis Cardinals in 1968 (305 innings pitched, 38 runs allowed). That's awesome.

Baseball Words and Terms

Assist—A throw made by a player that enables a teammate to make a putout.

At-bat—An official turn as a batter. (An at-bat is not charged when the batter receives a base on balls, is hit by a pitched ball, is interfered with by an opposing player, or hits a sacrifice bunt or fly.)

Balk—An illegal motion by the pitcher meant to deceive a base runner.

Base on Balls—A free passage to first base given to a batter who receives four pitches outside the strike zone at which he does not swing.

Boxscore—The record of play of a game.

Bullpen—A fenced-off area, usually beyond the outfield fence, where relief pitchers warm up during the game.

Bunt—A batted ball that is tapped lightly.

Chance—The opportunity to catch or field a batted ball and make a putout. A chance results in a putout, assist, or error.

Designated Hitter—A player who bats in the lineup, usually in place of the pitcher, but does not play in the field.

Doubleheader—Two games held one after the other on the same day.

Double Play—A play in which two players are put out.

Dugout—A roofed structure, usually below ground level, where the players sit during a game.

Earned Run—A run scored before the third putout of the inning and for which the pitcher is responsible.

Error—A misplay by a fielder that allows a batter to be safe or a runner to advance.

Fair Ball—A batted ball that lands between the foul lines, or that is between the foul lines when bounding past first or third base or when it clears the outfield fence.

Force Play—A situation in which the runner must attempt to reach the next base because the batter has hit a fair ball.

Foul Ball—A batted ball that lands outside the foul lines or that is outside the foul lines when it passes first or third base.

Foul Tip—A foul ball that caroms straight back and is caught by the catcher.

Hit—A batted ball that is hit into fair territory that enables the batter to reach first base safely without aid of an error, a force play, or an attempt to put out a base runner.

Inning—A division of a game in which each team gets a turn at bat.

Passed Ball—A pitched ball that the catcher is expected to catch but misses, and that enables a runner to advance.

Pennant—The league championship.

Perfect Game—A no-hitter in which no opposing batter reaches first base.

Pinch-hitter—A player who is sent to bat in place of another player.

Pitcher's Mound—The elevated portion of the playing field between home plate and second base where the pitcher winds up to deliver the ball.

Pitcher's Rubber—See Rubber

Pitchout—A pitch thrown too wide for the batter to hit and which is intended to give the catcher a chance to throw out a runner trying to steal.

Putout—The act of putting a player out. The player who tags out a runner, catches a fly ball, or touches a base on a force play is credited with a putout.

Quick Pitch—A pitch thrown before the batter is ready.

RBI—Abbreviation for runs (or run) batted in.

Relief Pitcher—A pitcher who replaces another during a game.

Rookie—A first-year player.

Rubber—The rectangular slab of white rubber set crosswise in the pitcher's mound.

Run—One point, scored each time a player circles the bases and touches home plate.

Run Batted In—A run that scores as a result of a hit, a base on balls, or other offensive action by the batter.

Sacrifice—A bunt on which the batter is put out that serves to advance a base runner.

Sacrifice Fly—A fly ball caught for an out that is long enough to permit a runner to tag up and score.

Save—The credit given to a relief pitcher who enters a game with his team in the lead and preserves the lead for the remainder of the game.

Shutout—A victory in which one team is prevented from scoring.

Steal—To break for and reach the next base safely without the batter hitting the ball.

Strike—A pitched ball at which the batter swings and misses, hits foul, or which crosses home plate within the strike zone, and is charged to the batter.

Strike Zone—The area through which the ball must pass to be ruled a strike.

Switch Hitter—A batter who is able to bat both left-handed and right-handed.

Tag Up—To stay in contact with a base on a fly ball with the idea of advancing to the next base after the ball is caught.

Triple Crown—Leading one's league for the season in batting average, runs batted in, and home runs.

Triple Play—A play in which three players are put out.

Unearned Run—A run scored as a result of an error or through interference by the catcher. Also, a run scored after the team in the field has had an opportunity to make the third out of an inning.

Walk—To receive a base on balls.

Wild Pitch—A pitched ball that the catcher misses and could not be expected to catch, and which results in a runner's advance.

Winning Pitcher—The pitcher on the winning team who is given credit in the official records for the victory.

All-time Major League Leaders

GAMES

Pete Rose	3,562
Carl Yastrzemski	3,308
Hank Aaron	3,298
Ty Cobb	3,033
Stan Musial	3,026
Willie Mays	2,992
Rusty Staub	2,951
Brooks Robinson	2,896
Al Kaline	2,834
Eddie Collins	2,826

HITS

Pete Rose	4,256
Ty Cobb	4,191
Hank Aaron	3,771
Stan Musial	3,630
Tris Speaker	3,515
Honus Wagner	3,430
Carl Yastrzemski	3,419
Eddie Collins	3,309
Willie Mays	3,283
Nap Lajoie	3,252

AT-BATS

Pete Rose	14,043
Hank Aaron	12,364
Carl Yastrzemski	11,988
Ty Cobb	11,429
Stan Musial	10,972
Willie Mays	10,881
Brooks Robinson	10,654
Honus Wagner	10,427
Lou Brock	10,332
Luis Aparicio	10,230

HOME RUNS

Hank Aaron	755
Babe Ruth	714
Willie Mays	660
Frank Robinson	586
Harmon Killebrew	573
Reggie Jackson	563
Mickey Mantle	536
Jimmie Foxx	534
Mike Schmidt*	530
Ted Williams	521

* Active player

RUNS

Ty Cobb	2,245
Hank Aaron	2,174
Babe Ruth	2,174
Pete Rose	2,165
Willie Mays	2,062
Stan Musial	1,949
Lou Gehrig	1,888
Tris Speaker	1,881
Mel Ott	1,859
Frank Robinson	1,829

STRIKEOUTS

Nolan Ryan*	4,547
Steve Carlton	4,131
Tom Seaver	3,640
Gaylord Perry	3,534
Don Sutton	3,530
Walter Johnson	3,508
Phil Niekro	3,342
Bert Blyleven*	3,286
Ferguson Jenkins	3,192
Bob Gibson	3,117

RUNS BATTED IN

Hank Aaron	2,297
Babe Ruth	2,204
Lou Gehrig	1,990
Ty Cobb	1,961
Stan Musial	1,951
Jimmie Foxx	1,922
Willie Mays	1,903
Mel Ott	1,860
Carl Yastrzemski	1,844
Ted Williams	1,839

STOLEN BASES

Lou Brock	938
Ty Cobb	892
Eddie Collins	743
Max Carey	738
Honus Wagner	703
Rickey Henderson*	701
Joe Morgan	689
Bert Campaneris	631
Maury Wills	586
Davey Lopes*	557

* Active player

Index

Strikes and Balls, 38, 39, 51, 53; how
  scored, 39
Substitutes, 62
Sutton, Don, 36

Tagging drills, *64*
Television, 99; W2XBS, 101
Tennessee Tanning Company of Tulla-
  homa, Tennessee, 24
Third baseman, 12
Thornton, Lou, 64
Training camp, *17, 72*
Triple Crown Award, 84, *85*
Triple play, 65; unassisted play, 65
Toronto Blue Jays, *31, 61, 64*

Umpires, 38, 51, 52, 53, 62, 103
Uniforms, 28, 30

Valenzuela, Fernando, 44
Vance, Dazzy, 80

Walk, 39, 40; intentional, 40
Wilhelm, Hoyt, 45
Williams, Ted, 110, *111*
World champion, 76
World Series, 51, 76, 77, 78, *78*, 79, 97,
  98, 99, 107
World War II, 79
Wright, Harry, 96

Yankee Stadium, *73*, 99
Yastremski, Carl, 84
Yeagher, Steve, 33
Young, Denton True (Cy), 81, 82

Zamboni water machine removal, 22

Courtesy of Ron Schwartz

George Sullivan is a free-lance writer known for his sports books. He is the author of over 100 non-fiction titles, which include *The Art of Base-Stealing, Pitchers and Pitching, Home Run!* and *Baseball's Wacky Players.*

Mr. Sullivan writes for both adults and young readers and, in response to requests from librarians, he prepared *All About Football*, a volume on football basics and highlights at the fourth grade reading level. Now he offers the game of baseball in a similar presentation.

George Sullivan was born in Lowell, Massachusetts, and was graduated from Fordham University. He lives in New York City.